YD

TALES FROM THE SOUTH PACIFIC ISLANDS

told by Anne Gittins

illustrated by Frank Rocca
jacket design by Tom Kealiinohomoku

1977

STEMMER
HOUSE
PUBLISHERS, INC.

Owings Mills, Maryland

Inquiries are to be directed to
STEMMER HOUSE PUBLISHERS, INC.
2627 Caves Road, Owings Mills,
Maryland 21117

A Barbara Holdridge Book
First Edition

Published simultaneously in Canada by George J. McLeod, Limited, Toronto

Printed and bound in the United States of America

Library of Congress Cataloging in Publication Data

Gittins, Anne.
  Tales from the South Pacific Islands.

   SUMMARY: Folk tales collected from Fiji, Rotuma, Tonga,
Samoa, the New Hebrides, and other South Pacific islands.
   1. Tales, Oceanian. [1. Folklore—Oceanica]
I. Rocca, Frank. II. Title.
GR380.G55   398.2'099   76-5411
ISBN 0-916144-02-X

Contents

Preface

Every country has its own folk tales, handed down from grandparents to children, often gaining a new twist or a different version with each telling. This is why there are many variations in the stories of the Pacific; for instance, the beautiful maiden in the story of the coconut tree may be Ina, Sina or Hina, depending on who is telling the tale.

In the old days the people of the Pacific had many gods and guardian spirits to protect them who were said to take the shapes of sharks, snakes or mythical giants. But when the missionaries arrived in the islands they told the people that they must put away these ideas and stories, and as a result, the children grew up without knowing their own folklore. Now the tales have been collected and are taught again in the island schools. And they can be enjoyed as well by children all over the world.

My husband was in the British Colonial Administrative Service when we went out to Fiji in 1930. The territory consists of about three hundred islands, some eighty of which are occupied, and they vary from tiny coral atolls to larger islands of volcanic origin. For this reason we traveled often, sailing in small twelve-ton cutters or schooners between the islands, or riding along the bush paths on unshod ponies. And so the tales came alive for us as we were watching the barefoot firewalkers, viewing the sacred red prawns, or listening to girls singing their very old songs as they called up the turtles from the sea.

When we went "on tour" we stayed in Fijian houses in the villages. And sometimes in the evenings we sat on the floor on mats around a flickering hurricane lantern, listening to the Fijians telling us the stories that had been woven around the sights we had seen. Some of these are now included in this book.

Anne Gittins

TALES
FROM THE
SOUTH PACIFIC
ISLANDS

HOW THE MOSQUITOES
CAME TO ONEATA

Among the islands that lie to the east of Fiji, there are two called Oneata and Kambara.

Long ago there were no mosquitoes on Oneata. But the Kambara people were sorely troubled and plagued by them. They were stung day and night and could find no rest, in spite of the unceasing work of their women, who pounded the paper-mulberry bark until their arms ached, to make mosquito curtains.

However, on Oneata there were plenty of shellfish with a particularly delicate flavor, which were found on the beaches and in caves, and the Kambara people were very envious as they had none. Listen now, and I will tell you how these things came to be changed.

Once, long ago, ten men of the boat-building tribe of Oneata were washed out to sea when a river overflowed its banks. They clung desperately to a tree trunk, and by and by they drifted to

Kambara. Afraid of being killed, they begged the chief to spare their lives and promised to work for him.

The chief, whose name was Tuwara, was a wise and cunning man, and he was very pleased to hear about the wonderful boats that they had built, strong enough to sail even in stormy weather. His own island was full of splendid trees, and so he set the men to work to build a great double canoe. In order to keep them happy he gave them houses, food and wives, so that they would not pine to return home.

The work lasted more than two years, for in those days there were no hatchets or saws. First of all, sharp stones and shells were used for cutting the logs. Then the hulls were hollowed out with burning brands and scraped, while the men used pointed shells or small firebrands for boring holes. Strong vines and cords of coconut fiber bound the body-work together, and the great sail was plaited from tough leaves.

When at last the canoe was finished it was dragged down to the sea, and the launching was celebrated with a feast.

Tuwara, impatient to put to sea, went on board, taking the carpenters as crew and a crowd of his people as well. Singing lustily, they sailed away with a light breeze filling the sail. But when the wind blew stronger and the canoe began to pitch and roll among the waves, the singers changed their tune to groans. They huddled together or lay clutching the deck, for they were all seasick.

"What is this terrible feeling, O carpenters?" moaned Tuwara. "What is this fearful sickness?"

The carpenters only laughed at the Kambara folk.

"Wait a little, sir, and then it will pass," they said. "It is always thus when you first put out to sea." But they were answered with fresh groans by the unhappy people.

Soon the outlines of Oneata appeared on the horizon.

"There is land ahead, sir. Shall we steer for it?" said Melani, the graybeard, the eldest of the boat-builders. "Or would you go still farther?"

"No, no, steer for it, and let us land," groaned Tuwara.

The people of Oneata had seen the canoe coming, and thinking that it was a huge sea monster they ran into the bush and hid, so that Tuwara found an empty town when he landed. He entered the chief's house and threw himself down on the mats to rest. Then the people slowly returned to the village, and when they had lost their fear of the strangers, they talked to them and heard their tale and looked with wonder at the canoe.

Tuwara stayed on this pleasant island many days, for he found the shellfish good to eat and his sleep was not disturbed by troublesome mosquitoes. When at last they sailed homeward they invited Wa-Kulikuli, the lord of Oneata, to come with them to see Kambara.

A great feast was prepared when they arrived, and after eating and drinking his fill, the Oneata chief began to yawn. Tuwara took him into his house, where a large mosquito curtain hung, and the visitor was surprised by the size of the curtain and by the beautiful patterns that were painted on it.

"What is this wonderful piece of cloth? We have nothing like it on our island. And why do you keep it hanging up in this manner?"

"Oh," said Tuwara, "it is useful as a screen, and it also protects me when the wind blows cold. Let us sleep now, and I will show you the village in the morning."

He lied about his curtain because he was ashamed of the mosquitoes, which were indeed a plague upon his island, and he hoped to deceive his friend. But when darkness fell, thousands of mosquitoes commenced to buzz outside the curtain, and the chief of Oneata was awakened.

"What sweet sound is that outside?" he asked.

Tuwara pretended that he had not heard and only answered with a snore.

"Eh! Wake up, tell me what those sweet noises are," the chief insisted.

This time Tuwara could no longer pretend to be asleep.

"Which sounds? Oh, those! They are only the mosquitoes buzzing," he replied with a yawn.

"What are mosquitoes?" asked his friend.

"They are little insects, and at night they fly about and buzz, and I keep them to sing me to sleep," said the crafty Tuwara. The Oneata chief begged to be allowed to take the little singers home with him.

"Give you my mosquitoes? Nay, I dare not; my people would never forgive me."

"Well, just give me some of them and keep the rest," pleaded Wa-Kulikuli.

"That, alas, is impossible, for if I give even a few away the rest will follow them and will leave me," said the cunning man. "I am indeed sad that I must refuse you, but now let us go to sleep."

Wa-Kulikuli continued to trouble his friend with his pleading. He and his people would always be grateful to Tuwara, he said, and would tell their children to love and respect him.

"That is a tempting thought, but I dare not give them away for *nothing*. What would my people say to me?"

"No, no, I will give you anything you care to ask for in return," said the Oneata chief. "Choose what you like from my island and it shall be yours, if only I may have your mosquitoes."

"Well," said Tuwara, "I will not ask for myself. I must think of my people—and the thought has just come to me that they would like your shellfish. That is just the very thing. Give me the shellfish and you may have the mosquitoes."

"With pleasure," said the other. "That is a good bargain. Now, will you lift up the curtain so that I can see them?"

Tuwara was then afraid that his friend might be bitten and repent of his bargain, so he refused to lift the curtain. He said that his little insects were modest and bashful and did not like to be gazed at, and therefore they came out only at night.

"Let us sleep now, for it is late," he begged. But neither of them slept much, for Wa-Kulikuli lay and listened to the song of the mosquitoes, and Tuwara chuckled over the good bargain he had made. He determined to prevent his friend from rising too early, lest a few insects still be flitting about. The foolish chief might realize the trick that he was about to play.

With the first streaks of dawn the Oneata chief called out, "Wake up, Tuwara. It is time for us to depart, so give me the mosquitoes."

"*Isa!* What a restless person you are," said the other. It is scarcely dawn, and you have kept me awake half the night with your talking. Lie still awhile, for at this hour the mosquitoes gather together and fly away to a cave where they sleep in the daytime. If we disturb them now we shall be unable to catch them."

"Very well, let us wait," said Wa-Kulikuli. But every few minutes he cried out again, "Do you think they are asleep yet?" and a little later, "Surely they are in their cave now?"—so eager he was to catch them! By this time Tuwara was indeed angry with the foolish chief and would gladly have hit him with his club. Only the thought of the shellfish made him keep his temper, and he did not rise until it was daylight.

"Come now, and let us sail to your land," he said.

No one saw him collect the mosquitoes, but by the time the canoe was ready he had shut them all in a large basket. This was lined inside and covered with fine mats, through which not even a small mosquito could crawl, and it was carried on board hastily.

Again they were seasick, but Wa-Kulikuli comforted himself with the thought of his little singers, and Tuwara was cheered with the hope of being rid of his plague, in exchange for the shellfish.

It was high noon when they landed at Oneata and furled their sails. Wa-Kulikuli, leaping ashore, called all his people to see what he had brought them, and he begged Tuwara to hand down the basket.

"Not so fast, my friend," said the cunning Tuwara. "My mosquitoes are a loving tribe, and if I let them go now they will not leave the canoe, for they love me and will not leave me. So give me your shellfish first. Then I will depart, leaving the basket here, and if you are wise you will not open it until I have sailed beyond the reef lest the mosquitoes fly after me."

"That is true, and you are wise, O Tuwara!" Then Wa-Kulikuli turned and gave a great shout—"Come, O shellfish, come from the beach and from the sea and from the rocks. It is your chief who calls."

Then from the shore, and from their homes in caves and pools, the shellfish crawled in by the hundreds. The men threw them into the canoe until it was full and shellfish were heaped high upon the deck, and not one was left upon the island.

"Now give me the basket and you may depart, for all the shellfish are on board," said the impatient chief. So Tuwara handed over the basket while his men hoisted the sail, and away they sailed with all speed.

The Oneata men now came crowding around to see what treasure their chief had brought them. It must surely be something of great value, or he would never have parted with their shellfish, they thought. Wa-Kulikuli waited until the canoe was clear of the reef, and then he untied the fastenings of the basket and lifted the mat.

Up rose the mosquitoes in a gray cloud, buzzing angrily, and

loudly the people screamed and yelled as they were bitten by the savage insects.

"Ha, ha, ha," laughed Tuwara, for he could hear the distant cries. "Wa-Kulikuli's sweet singers have already begun their song. Ho, ho, I have met many fools, but never such a fool as yonder chief."

The wretched lord of Oneata spent days and nights thinking of schemes to get rid of the plague of insects he had brought to his land, but alas, they increased in numbers every day. He made many plans to get back his shellfish, and after some years he sailed over to Kambara one night.

Standing on the beach he called them: "Come, my shellfish, it is I, your lord, who is calling." But not one of them heard him and not one returned to him.

But Tuwara heard him. He lay in wait and watched him. Then, creeping up quietly, he smote him on the head with his club and cried out, "O wretched man, would you steal my shell-fish?"

So Wa-Kulikuli, driven back to his canoe, returned sadly to his island and to his sweet singing plague of mosquitoes.

THE FIREWALKERS

On an island near Suva, the capital of Fiji, there lives a tribe known as the Firewalkers. The men walk on burning hot stones, and yet their feet are never burnt and their skin is not even singed.

The people say that long ago an ancestor of theirs was given the power to do this by a stranger, and from that day to this they have been able to walk on heated stones.

The men of the village used to meet in a large house in the evenings to chat and to tell stories. Each one took turns in providing food, and they always tried to bring some special delicacy for their evening meal.

One day a man called King Chestnut Tree promised to catch some eels; so he set off very early in the morning and went to fish in a small pool. There he found that a large stone had fallen into the water, making it very muddy. So he climbed onto the stone and sat down, thinking that perhaps a big fish was hiding beneath it. He began to dig around the stone with a stick, and then he jumped down into the hole he had made, and very cautiously he felt with his hand. Suddenly he pulled out a great eel.

He threw the creature across his shoulder and started to return home with his fine contribution to the feast. But he had not gone very far when his burden spoke to him. "Do not kill me," he said. "Spare my life, and if you let me go I will give you wealth and riches."

The eel slipped off his shoulder and immediately turned into a fine young man.

"I don't need wealth, for I am already rich," replied Chestnut Tree. "Who are you?"

"My name is King Lemonjuice," said the young man. "Please let me live and in return I will make you the champion javelin thrower."

"All my tribe are javelin throwers, and I happen to be their captain," said Chestnut Tree proudly.

"Let me live," begged Lemonjuice, and he tried to bribe his captor by offering to make him the most handsome man, and then the best navigator. But Chestnut Tree became tired of this bargaining and refused all the tempting offers.

"I will teach you how to walk on hot stones and bear terrific heat," promised the captive, who was becoming desperate.

"What was that? What did you say?" Chestnut Tree was interested at last.

Lemonjuice explained quickly that the first task was to gather firewood for four days. Then they must dig a large pit.

"Then we must light a fire in the pit, and after that we must bury ourselves in the embers and bake for four days and four nights. When we have done that I shall have kept the promise I made to you in return for sparing my life, and we can both go home."

Chestnut Tree agreed to do this, and together they made a great oven and heated the stones with fire for four days and nights. When the embers were removed and the stones leveled, the two men walked over the burning hot stones and then stepped onto the grass once more. Neither of them had singed a foot or burnt a toe, nor had they any pain or discomfort.

Lemonjuice suggested that they should bury themselves in the oven, but his friend was afraid that this might be a trick and that he would be left there to be cooked alive.

"No, I prefer just to step on the stones and not stay there long lest my skirt be burnt," he said.

So he did that again and came out of the oven safely without a burn, and from that day to this all the men of that tribe have been able to walk on hot stones as their ancestor did long ago.

TUI LIKU AND
THE DEMONS

In olden days there were times when the small isle of Ono suffered severe droughts. It lay among the Lau islands, a scattered chain of small islands that lie between Fiji and Tonga, and so its people could always sail over to Tuvana, which was a day's journey. Although Tuvana was uninhabited, it was rich and fertile, and said to be near to the spirit-land of the gods.

One day a number of men and women from the town of Matokano on Ono sailed to Tuvana in a large canoe to gather coconuts and other food. Arriving there at sunset, hungry and tired, they collected food quickly and cooked it, and then found a rough shelter in which to sleep, at a place called Butoni. During the night the wind freshened, and by morning a gale was blowing, and the men debated whether they should leave the women there and return to Ono with all the rest of the food they had gathered, since it was needed urgently.

There was one whose name was Tui Liku, a handsome high-

14

spirited man and a great favorite with the girls. Having listened to the discussion, he decided on a plan of his own, hoping to be left behind as well.

"I will collect food at once," he said, and went off into the bush and hid.

The other men also filled their baskets with food and stored them in the canoe, and then, since Tui Liku appeared to be lost, they hoisted the sail and prepared to depart. Just as they were leaving the shore Tui Liku came out of his hiding place and hurried along, but not too fast, with his basket full of rubbish. He called out to the men, but they only laughed at him. Then to his horror he saw that the women had embarked as well, and that now he was to be left quite alone on the island.

"Come back, come back," he shouted, but they laughed again, for they had suspected his trick and intended to leave him behind.

He sat and watched the canoe as it sailed away, growing smaller and smaller in the distance. Then he cooked some food, and with a heavy heart he lay down to sleep in the shelter.

In the night he woke suddenly, hearing voices. He thought that his friends had returned after all to fetch him. Since he could see no one, he called out to them, but only a mocking laugh answered him, and he heard the voices speaking in a strange tongue. By now he was terrified and crept to the wall of the hut, trying to hide in the dark shadows.

"Eh! Tui Liku," called a strange voice, "we have come for you."

Tui Liku shook with fright, for he knew now that these were the demons of Tuvana. And then he was seized by strong hands and dragged out of the shelter into the moonlight.

The leader of the gang was a little humpbacked man. He snatched up the frightened lad and threw him to one of the others, who tossed him up into the air and caught him again, laughing loudly. Then the rest took their turns at tossing him and playing catch, like a crowd of children, all through the night.

When daylight came the leader said, "Go and sleep now, Tui Liku. We will not kill you this time, for we shall come and play with you again tonight."

Wearily Tui Liku crawled back to the little house and lay down, and the spirits fled. He slept awhile, and when he woke up he tried to think of a cunning plan to outwit the little men. He ate some food and then went out to collect firewood, and he brought great bundles, arranging them in a ring around the outside of the house.

"Demons will not venture across fire," he said to himself, and when darkness descended he set fire to his wood and went inside and lay down peacefully.

He had not slept long before he was awakened by a shrill laugh and heard a hissing sound. He peeped through a crack in the reed wall, and he saw that the little men had brought water from the sea in banana leaves, and they had put out the fire on one side. Again he tried to creep away, but the leader seized him by the leg and tossed him out to the others. All night long they played toss with him and disappeared again at sunrise.

Tui Liku was very worried and all that day he brooded over another plan. At night he climbed up into a high coconut tree and settled himself to sleep among its large leaves, for he was weary from lack of rest.

Before long he was awakened again by the demons laughing, and he heard them running up and down the shore looking for him. By and by one of them started to climb up his tree to fetch a coconut for a drink, and Tui Liku shook with fright. Higher and higher climbed the demon. Then he saw Tui Liku, and with a loud yell he plucked him out and flung him down to the rest, who were waiting for their nightly game of toss.

Tui Liku was nearly dead by the morning but managed to

crawl to the hut at Butoni, for he needed sleep badly, and he slept till the sun was high overhead. Then he cracked some nuts and drank the milk and scraped others, rubbing his poor bruised body with oil, while he thought of a new idea for the night.

"If I hide anywhere on land those demons will find me," he thought. "Ah! Perhaps if I cut down a coconut tree by the water's edge and let the top of it lie with its leaves in the sea, rising and falling with the tide, the demons may be unable to pass over the water."

So he carried out his plan, and this time he hoped for a good rest as he hid among the thick leaves, for this was the fourth night he had passed on the haunted island, with scarcely any sleep since he had come.

His trick was almost successful, for it was nearly midnight before the sound of their voices wakened him. They were angry now as they searched here and there, thinking that he must have escaped them and sailed away. But their leader suddenly came across the fresh-cut tree stump, and with a shout he ran along the trunk and caught Tui Liku by the hair and pulled him out.

That night was not so long, but Tui Liku was weary and discouraged by the failure of his last plan, and he could think of nothing new.

Next day he sat and rubbed his aching limbs and watched the little sand crabs, the Kaiki, as they scurried along the beach and hid in their holes.

"I have tried the land, the air and the water. This time I think I will follow the example of the Kaiki," he said. So he dug a deep hole, and at dusk he buried himself, leaving only a small hole to breathe through.

This time the demons could find no trace of him, and Tui Liku hoped that he had fooled them. They were about to give up their search when the leader said, "Let us have something to eat. We will all catch some Kaiki for supper."

Now the way to catch crabs for fish bait is to prod their holes with a stick, and the demons went up and down the sand seeking for the little crab holes. Just then the leader found Tui Liku's hole.

"*Sombo!*" he said. "Here is a large one!" And he put his arm down the hole and caught Tui Liku by the nose and pulled him out.

That night the demons played a new game. They raced along the beach dragging the unhappy man around and around the island and often through the water. By morning he thought his end was near, and he was thrown inside the small house and left to himself.

Most of that day he slept, and later he ate a little food. He thought sadly of his people in the town of Matokano and wished they would come back and fetch him, for there was nowhere else to hide. Thinking of his friends gave him a fresh idea, and he went out and cut down five large stems of banana trees and brought them into the house. He cut them to the length of men and put them on the floor to look like sleeping people, and then he lay down between them.

When darkness fell he heard the voices as usual, and one demon came to the door and looked through a crack.

"*Sombo!* The others must have returned," he said, thinking the banana stems were slumbering men.

Tui Liku heard them whispering together outside, and then they began to sing, changing their voices to sound like maidens. He had never heard such sweet songs before, or such sweet tones. On and on they sang till Tui Liku sat up in order to listen more easily.

Then one who had been hiding by the door cried out, "See, there is Tui Liku. The others are not men of this world or they would not lie still and sleep while we sing. This is just one more of his tricks."

Rushing into the house, they dragged him outside. That night they were more violent than ever and threw him about from one end of the island to the other till he could scarcely move.

"Another night like that and there will be no more Tui Liku," he murmured to himself. He lay down on his mat and tried to sleep after the demons had left him more dead than alive. He slept until the afternoon, and then he oiled his aching limbs while his head nodded with weariness.

Suddenly there appeared before him one of the lords of the spirit-land, Lingandua the one-armed, who was the protector of the Matokano people. He asked Tui Liku what had happened and why he was so sad.

"It is the demons of this place, my lord," he said. "They have almost killed me." And he related all the pranks they had played on him each night.

Lingandua was filled with wrath, and he strode over to the great drum that stood near his own house. He beat loudly upon it, and presently all the demons came running to him and sat down in a circle.

Lingandua then told them that he was very angry, and he bade them leave Tui Liku alone and never touch him again. They bowed their heads in silence and plucked at the grass to show that they were ashamed, and one by one they crept away.

Then Lingandua called Tui Liku, bidding him wait in his own big house till the Matokano people came back for him.

"It is now time for me to return to Burotu, the spirit-land," he said.

Tui Liku asked if he might be allowed to see this land.

"Nay," replied Lingandua, "if I take your spirit with me it might not be able to return again into its body, for no man of the world has ever yet come back from that land."

The young man continued to plead, so at length Lingandua

consented to take him. "You must follow my footsteps and do whatever I tell you, or you will never again return to earth," he said as he led the way down to the beach. The waves were rolling in over the reef, and Lingandua cautioned him to take no notice of white ones but that when a red wave came he was to jump, for that was the ferryboat to the spirit-land.

"Come over to us, O chiefly canoe," he called, looking toward the deep sea. He explained that, as the chief's canoes were made of the red vesi wood, the ferry-wave was therefore also a red color. Then a red wave came with white spray flying. They both jumped into it, but only the spirit of Tui Liku went over to Burotu with Lingandua, while his body was washed back onto the shore.

When they reached the spirit-land they came to a town with fine houses and a great council house. Here Lingandua's father sat in state, for he was the king.

Then there were ceremonies of welcome and a feast, and the people brought presents to the king's son. Tui Liku was forbidden to enter the houses or to make friends with the maidens, but he was allowed to take some red coconuts back to Tuvana to plant.

Four times Tui Liku went over to the spirit-land in the same manner, and he took back nuts, seeds and a little bird that flits among the coconut trees. On returning to Tuvana the fourth time, he was dismayed to see that a sandpiper had been pecking at his body as it lay on the shore, and that it had pecked out one eye.

"*Isa!* I refuse to get back into that body again," he cried, for he was a vain man and proud of his appearance.

"You must, for you may not stay here," said Lingandua.

So Tui Liku returned into his body, and it was not long before the canoe sailed over from Matokano to take him back to his own people; but forever after he was known as the One-Eyed, and the sandpipers on Tuvana island still call, "Tui Liku, Tui Liku," all day long, in honor of the man who planted the land with beauty.

THE DRUM THAT
LOST ITS VOICE

In days gone by there was much fighting among the people of the Lau islands. There were many raids on the villages, plantations were ruined, canoes were smashed, and houses were burned. So the people fled to hilltop forts, where they could keep watch for the coming of enemies.

At that time there was a great chief, called Tui Matokano, who lived on the island of Ono. Although he was the most powerful chief in those parts, he felt distressingly powerless at the sight of so much destruction, and above all he was troubled at losing his great village drum.

His island had no fine timber trees with which to make new canoes and a new drum, so he decided that his people must obtain canoes and a drum from another island by trading their own homemade goods.

He called all the villagers together and said, "Listen to me! We need new canoes, big ones for long journeys and small ones

22

for fishing. We need bowls, and we need a drum, big enough so that its voice will be heard for many miles across the water when we beat out messages.

"Go and weave fine mats, and beat the pulp of the paper-mulberry tree and make tapa cloth, and stencil it with beautiful designs, for we go to Kambara island."

So the women set to work and plaited fine mats, some for the floor and some for sleeping on, and they made quantities of tapa cloth, and when all was ready the men set off in their old canoes and arrived at Kambara.

Here they were successful with their bartering, obtaining four canoes and many bowls and a fine big drum made of rich vesi wood. This drum was half as high as a man and polished smooth, and the sound it made when struck with mallets was like thunder that echoed over the land.

The men from Ono waited some time for a favorable wind. Finally it was possible to return home, but first a farewell feast was prepared. Then with sails set they steered for Ono.

As darkness began to fall a storm blew up and the curling waves dashed over the canoes, and they were all afraid. Throughout the night the balers never ceased to bale, but the wind blew stronger and the waves mounted higher and higher.

"Throw over an offering of kava for One-Arm, the god of our village. We are in great danger, and he alone can save us," shouted Tui Matakano above the roar of the wind.

"If we should reach the shores of Ono safely, I will make a chiefly feast and give presents to him as a thank-offering," he promised.

Before long the fierce winds and waves died down, and as dawn broke the exhausted men saw the hilltops of their own island.

There was much rejoicing when the villagers saw the fine things the men had brought from Kambara. But then Tui Matokano went off to plant yams in his garden, and he forgot all about his promise to the god.

But One-Arm had not forgotten. He waited for his feast and grew impatient, and he decided that Tui Matokano must be taught a lesson.

So one evening at dusk he strode into the village when the people had finished their day's work and were sitting on the village green and resting. No one recognized him as, with eyes flashing, he walked boldly up to the great new drum that stood in front of Tui Matokano's house. With one hand grasping the drum he looked at the chief, who saw that this stranger had only one arm. Suddenly he was filled with fear and shame, and he remembered the promise he had made in the storm.

One-Arm looked around at all the people. Then, laughing loudly, he flew off, grasping something in his hand that looked like the gray shadow of the drum.

Presently the villagers who had bowed their heads in fear looked up, and they saw that their prized possession was still standing in its usual place.

"*Sombo!* I must have fallen asleep and had a bad dream," said Tui Matokano, shaking his head. "It seems to me that it would be a good thing if we made a feast for our god, now that I come to think of it."

He told a man near him to beat the drum to summon everyone to discuss the preparation of the feast. So the man picked up the two mallets and started to beat the call, but not a sound was heard. He looked at the mallets in his hand, and then at the wooden drum, and he tried again. Still no hollow booming was heard. In terror the man threw down his mallets and fled.

"Fool, why don't you do as I tell you?" shouted Tui Matokano, who by now was very angry.

He went across the green himself and tried to beat the drum. There was no sound but the chirping of the cicadas and the distant roll of the surf. The people watched him anxiously as he sat down, and then in the silence they heard a faraway sound coming from over the water. It was like the voice of their great drum, and as they listened it seemed to mock them.

The great drum never spoke again. But often on a calm night the people thought they heard its voice in the distance, and they lamented that all their efforts in bringing it to their island had been in vain.

A FIJIAN FABLE

Everyone loves a feast, and the birds, beasts and insects are no exception.

One day the frog, the grasshopper, the land crab, the sandpiper bird, the tree spider and the bull ant all met together and decided to have a feast.

"Each one must do his share to help," said the sandpiper. "I, being a fisherman, will bring fish." And off he flew to the beach and began to wade among the small pools left by the tide to see what he could find.

"I will bring nuts for a vegetable," chirruped the grasshopper, and with a great hop he went off to climb an ivi tree in search of its delicious nuts.

"I have strong and powerful claws that are useful for digging," said the crab, "so I will dig out the hollow pit for the oven, and I will bring stones for lining it."

The ant went to break off branches to cover the food in the

oven, but in climbing up a breadfruit tree she stuck to the sticky gum on the bark and there she died.

The grasshopper, in trying to bite off the stem of an ivi nut, broke all his teeth and descended sadly to the ground, where he also died.

"Ha, ha! That is very funny," laughed the spider, and he slapped his thighs so hard that he broke them both. Then the frog shook with laughter at this mishap, and he puffed himself up and up till he burst.

The crab had been digging away all this time. He had almost finished the oven pit, but he had chosen a place with too many stones, and in trying to move a heavy one, he broke his claws and was therefore quite helpless.

Meanwhile the sandpiper had been the lucky one and had caught plenty of fish. He returned feeling well pleased with himself, only to find that his friends had each come to grief and that there was no one left. Without friends to share the feast, he found no enjoyment in dining on the fish he had worked so hard to catch.

WHY THE MOON HAS
SHADOWS ON HER FACE

There was once a god named Takei, and it was the custom for people to bring him offerings of fish. One day, being angry at having so small a quantity of fish presented to him, he made up his mind to ensnare the moon and extinguish her light by splashing her with salt water. This would be a great hindrance to the fishermen, who often went fishing by moonlight.

When his mother heard of his intention she was very upset, and she determined to do all she could to prevent such a calamity. She knew it would be useless to oppose her son openly, so she moaned and cried as if the thought of this plan filled her with great grief.

"Oh, what will the king of Rewa do when he orders his fishermen to go afishing?" she wailed. "There will be no midnight lamp for them. And what will the king of Bau do? There will be no light for either his fishermen or for the king of Nayau's men."

In the midst of all this lamentation she managed artfully to get hold of the long bamboos that the god had filled with sea water in order to destroy the moon. Pouring off the salt, she refilled the bamboos with fresh water and replaced them without being seen, and she chuckled to herself at the thought of outwitting her son.

Takei then ordered a trap to be prepared. It was made from the branches of a gigantic tree, and very large, and baited with most tempting food.

By and by crowds of spectators arrived, all eager to see what would happen. As the moon, full of curiosity, left her usual position in the sky and came lower and lower toward the trap, the people held their breath with excitement. When at last the moon was caught, Takei ran up with his bamboos, thinking that he would put out her light forever with the salt water.

He was indeed surprised and very angry to find that the water did not harm her at all, and that she managed to escape from his snare.

It seems that the moon, accustomed all her life to rain, was unharmed by the fresh water, as Takei's old mother knew full well. The dark places on her surface, the people say, are the smears of mud that were left on her while she was in the trap and have remained there ever since.

THE RED PRAWNS
OF VATU-LÉLÉ

Long ago there lived on the little island of Vatu-Lélé a very beautiful princess who was called the Maiden-of-the-Fair-Wind. She was so beautiful that her fame spread far and wide and every prince wished that she would become his queen.

Many princes sailed over to her island home to ask for her hand in marriage, but she refused them all. Then one day a young prince, renowned for his great strength, decided to try and win her love. He picked up some great rocks and threw them into the sea, making steppingstones from the main island to Vatu-Lélé; and taking giant strides he crossed over the sea to her home. In his haste he forgot to take any fine gifts for the princess, and he carried with him only a bundle of cooked prawns wrapped in leaves.

When he arrived at the little island he was taken to the palace, and when he saw the Maiden-of-the-Fair-Wind he fell in love with her immediately. He praised her beauty and asked her

30

to marry him, but she refused him, as she had refused many suitors before, and chased him out of the palace. Angry at the mean present of prawns he had brought, she threw the bundle after him. As it landed on the ground the bundle burst, spilling the cooked prawns into a pool with the leaves strewn around it.

As soon as the prawns touched the water they came to life again, but they remained as red as they had been before and never again returned to their transparent gray color. The leaves took root and grew among the crevices in the rocks, where they are still found by those who search for them.

In the course of time these prawns became sacred, and no one was allowed to touch them. It is said that anyone unwise enough to try and take some away will be shipwrecked.

THE GUARDIANS
OF THE ISLANDS

Long ago there were many powerful ancestral spirits who lived among the islands or in the waters around the reef. Sometimes they took the form of men and at other times they appeared as creatures, birds or fishes. And they were treated with great respect by the people.

The greatest of all was Dengei. He was the spirit of one of the first ancestors to arrive in Fiji, and the founder of many tribes. He was also the god of snakes, and he slept in a rocky cave high up on a mountain range on the largest island. Once in a while, however, he became restless and turned over in his sleep, and then the earth trembled, and when the noise rolled down from the mountaintop the people said that it thundered.

He disliked his sleep being disturbed, and he banished the bats that twittered in caves in his mountain. Even the noise of the surf as it pounded upon the reef annoyed him, and so he silenced it along one stretch of the coast. As for the pottery makers who beat their clay bowls and ovens in the villages, he removed them by putting out one foot and pushing their land into the sea, where it became two islands. So then he slept more peacefully and guarded the many spirits that passed along the mountain range on their way to the home of all departed spirits.

In the ocean, the most powerful deity was a great shark named Pursuer-of-Boats. He swam to and fro among the islands and fought and conquered most of the guardian spirits that protected the openings in the reef. But there was one who was more cunning than he, and this was a giant octopus who lurked around Kandavu island.

One day, fresh from defeating several monsters, Pursuer-of-Boats set out to battle with this enemy. Now the octopus knew he was coming, for he had seen his fin above the water, and therefore he had time to prepare. Stretching four of his tentacles to the bottom of the sea to secure a firm grip, and the other four to the surface of the water, he made a great barrier in the way of the shark's progress.

"Make way there, I am coming," sang out Pursuer-of-Boats as he came closer and closer, but the octopus grasped him and almost squeezed him to death. So tight was his grip that the shark could not free himself. Seeing that his life was in danger, he begged the octopus to let him go.

"If you will spare my life," he gasped, "I promise that in the future I will not harm any people from Kandavu, wherever they may be."

"Ah, now that is really a good bargain," said the octopus. "That is something worthwhile." And he unwound his tentacles and let the shark go free.

Pursuer-of-Boats then went on his way, rather subdued at first, but still ready to fight with any monster ready to stand up to him. The battles at times caused such a commotion at sea that tidal waves came rushing up the rivers and overflowed the low-lying deltas. He had a softer side to his nature, however, for he befriended the people of the northern island and even piloted their canoes when they were out on night raids, the phosphorescent glow of his wake serving as a guiding light.

So much for the legends of this monster of the deep! But like the stories of Moby Dick and other such creatures, they are often founded on fact; and the truth is that many a mariner has seen Pursuer-of-Boats and had a strange encounter with him. At times he has been described as a great shark, between thirty and fifty feet long, and at other times as a giant ray whose side flaps could envelop a small boat and cause it to sink. Yet another tale is told of a monster that clasped an eighteen-foot sailing boat with its fins and carried it back and forth on its back all day long, until at sundown an elderly Fijian promised it a gift of kava, a drink made from the root of a plant, if only it would release the boat and allow the crew to land. This promise must have pleased the creature, for it let go of the boat and contentedly swam away.

The snake and the shark are now legendary heroes, but there are sacred turtles actually to be seen to this day.

If you should sail to the islands of Koro and Kandavu and make an offering to the people, they will call their turtles up from the depths of the ocean. If you ask for an explanation as to why the turtles rise, the people of Kandavu will tell you this ancient story:

Long ago some chiefs went poaching, to catch fish in waters that did not belong to their tribe. On the way they saw two women, a mother and her beautiful daughter, and they caught them and carried them off in their boat. But the women immediately turned themselves into turtles. Seeing this, the men were filled with fear, and they threw their captives overboard. The turtles swam away, turning back into women as they reached the shore.

Even now the maidens of one village climb to the summit of a hill and there, overlooking the sea, they sing a song and chant. Before long two turtles swim up from beneath the rocks and coral and float on the surface of the water, listening. The rhythm of the singing and the clapping quickens until the turtles dive downward once more and only the waves that lap the rocks are left to disturb the deep blue water of the bay.

On the island of Koro a different legend is told about the turtles. Here, also, they are called up from the deep water by the people of one village who chant an ancient song until the turtles rise to the surface and swim ashore.

The elders say that it was the law in the olden days that all members of this village should go away from the place as soon as the turtle ceremony was over, and not return until the following day. They were warned that if they failed to obey this law some evil would overtake them.

Now long ago there was one man who scoffed at the ancient law, and one day he decided to wait until his friends had returned to their homes, to see what happened after the turtles came ashore. So when the singing was over he slipped away without being noticed and hid among the mangrove bushes until everyone had departed. After a while, since nothing happened, he came out from his hiding place and peered about cautiously, just in time to see a figure rise from the water and come toward the land. The figure, cloaked in mist, walked slowly along the beach. Quaking with fear, the man followed silently behind, hoping to find out where the mysterious figure was going; but after only a few moments the stranger turned and saw him.

"Rash and foolish man," he said, "you have not listened to the elders. You have broken the law and followed me; therefore you shall be punished. As a lesson to others, you shall be turned into a tree, and the seeds of it shall resemble a turtle. Those seeds will serve always as a reminder to people who are of a disbelieving nature."

Then the figure disappeared, and where the man had stood a tree appeared and quickly grew. In time, all who saw the fruit were filled with wonder, for the hard shells of the seeds closely resembled the back of a turtle. And to this day trees like that one grow and flourish on the island of Koro.

KOROIKA AND
THE SERPENT

During the months of October through December, which is mid-summer in the islands, the Lord of Life, god of the crops and harvest, came to earth each year, and as soon as he arrived the fruit trees blossomed and bore fruit. While he was on earth he turned himself into a serpent. He lived in a large cave near the island of Mbau, and the people went there to leave presents for him and to pay homage.

During those months all men were forbidden to make any noise lest they disturb the god, for if he were annoyed he might cause the crops to fail and bring about a famine. So they could not blow their conch shells or beat their drums. Neither could they sing or dance, and they were forbidden to fight or to cultivate their land.

Now there was a chief whose name was Koroika, and he would not believe in this god.

"I will go and find him and see him for myself," he said, and he set off in his canoe with a load of fresh fish.

As he neared the cave he was greeted by a fair-sized serpent, who said that he was the son of the god and asked what had brought him there.

"I have brought my gift according to custom and I crave an interview with your father," said Koroika, placing a basket of fish on the rocks.

Just then another serpent appeared. This was the god's grandson, and so he also received a present of fish, and he too was asked if his grandfather would deign to appear.

Koroika waited patiently and gazed into the dark mouth of the rocky cave, wondering if the god would really show himself. Then, gliding slowly, an immense serpent came out of the dim shadows, the largest one he had ever seen. Koroika bowed very low and presented a third offering of fish, which the god accepted graciously.

But just as the god turned to retreat into his cave, the treacherous Koroika shot him with an arrow. Then, suddenly filled with horror at his deed, he fled from the place. As he ran to his canoe he heard a terrible voice cry, "Naught but serpents! Naught but serpents!"

These ominous words were still ringing in his ears when he reached home.

"Bring me some food," he cried, hoping to forget his fear. But when his servants brought in the cooking pots and put them down they shrank back in horror, for out of the pots crawled serpents of all shapes and sizes.

"Then bring me water to drink," he called out, but as he raised the jar to his mouth out poured more serpents.

By now he was hungry and thirsty and very tired. Hoping to forget this nightmare, he threw himself onto his sleeping mat.

Then, from every corner of the house, hissing snakes came gliding toward him. The wretched man could get no sleep, and he fled from his house in terror.

The next morning, as he passed the village temple, he saw a crowd of people and heard the priest telling them that their god had been wounded by some dastardly fellow, and that unknown evils would befall the town before long.

Koroika's conscience caused him suddenly to tremble in every limb, and he realized that he could not conceal his crime. He then confessed that he was the culprit, and after making large offerings to please the angry god, he was pardoned.

WISEHEAD THE GIANT

Long ago there lived a giant who was taller than the tallest coconut tree. His name was Ulu-Matua, which means "Firstborn" or "Wisehead," and he lived on the second largest island in Fiji.

One day he decided to beautify his thick, curly hair, so he stirred up ashes and water in a clay pot and put the mixture on his head. Then he sat down in the sun and waited for it to dry. But the water kept on dripping from his hair. It dripped for days and days. Eventually two months passed, and it was still dripping.

This made his wife very angry. "What do you think you are doing, Wisehead?" she said. "All the women in the village are laughing at you, for you do no work. You neither tend your bananas nor plant your yams and dalo." So Wisehead rose and picked up his hardwood digging stick, which was twenty-four feet long and so heavy that only a giant could use it. But instead of going to work on his plantation he put the stick on his shoulder and carried it about day after day till he had walked up and down for two months!

41

This time his wife was really vexed. "Wisehead, I am ashamed of your behavior. You have planted nothing, and all the women are making fun of you," she scolded.

Then Wisehead went down to the beach to get away from the women. He found his canoe pulled up on the sand and he lay down in it, using his digging stick for a pillow. He had not slept for many days and so he was very weary. Before long the wind blew up and the rain came down in torrents, and there was a flood. The canoe broke away from its moorings—the vines that had tied it to a tree—and drifted away to sea. For three days and nights it drifted, until it came to rest on the beach of another island, and all this time Wisehead slept soundly.

At last, after two months, he awoke, sat up, and wondered where he was, for creepers were growing over him and over his canoe. Pushing these aside he stood up and looked for a path, and then he walked inland to find something to eat.

"There must be a village here, and if so there will be food," he said to himself.

It was not long before he came to some tall sugar cane, so he cut a stem and sucked the juice and walked on. Then he saw some tall pawpaw trees with ripe fruit as big as pumpkins, and picking twenty of the best he sat down in the shade and ate them all.

"That is much better," he said, and continued to walk along a narrow path. Next he came to some wild bananas, and he pulled down a great bunch and devoured them with one gulp. He then went on more cautiously, for he realized that there must be villagers nearby who came to tend these plantations.

Now the chief of that place had three children, a boy and twin girls, and that very day he had sent the girls to pick ripe bananas. Wisehead saw them coming, and not wishing to frighten them he turned himself into a little boy and ran about among the banana plants. He was now so small that he was unable to reach the hanging bunches of fruit, even though he jumped for them.

"Look here," called out one girl to her sister. "I have found a strange child. Where can he have come from? He is not from our island, for his hair is as white as the feathers of a heron!"

Wisehead did not look around but went on jumping for bananas, so the girls whistled to him to attract his attention. Then, pretending to be frightened, he sat down and began to cry.

"Oh, do not cry," said one of the girls. "Tell us where you come from."

"This must be a real child and not a demon, or it would have vanished," said the other.

Then they took him to their home and gave him food. And since he appeared to have no parents, they adopted him. The child grew fond of the twins and called them both "Mother" and followed them everywhere.

One day while he was out fishing on the reef with them, the child saw a turtle floating in the water.

"What is that?" he asked. "Can one eat it?"

"It is fine food," one of his new "mothers" replied. "It is food for chiefs."

"Well, let us catch it and kill it for your father, for he is a chief," said the child.

"You cannot catch it," she said, laughing, "and it is difficult to kill."

Taking up a rock, the child threw it and hit the turtle on the shell, and it sank down to the bottom of the sea and crawled along on the sand.

"See, I have killed it," he shouted, full of pride. But soon afterward he was surprised to see it coming ashore farther up the beach. He ran to it and jumped on its back and sat there laughing and singing.

"Take care, it will bite you," cried the "mother," who was afraid.

"No, no, it is not a turtle now, it is only a rock," the child replied, laughing, for the creature had hidden its head and flippers in the sand. Just then it raised its head a little, and when the child saw the eyes he was afraid and ran away, up the sandy beach. His "mother" cut creepers from the bush and called to her sister to help bind the turtle, and they tied it up.

Then the village people came and killed it, and there was much talk of a feast. But as they talked one man looked out to the sea and cried, "Ho! Look yonder! There are strange canoes coming over the waves," and they all fled back to the village in terror, forgetting about the turtle.

A single canoe then sailed into the bay and anchored, and a spokesman came ashore. He strode boldly to the chief's house and put down five whale's teeth upon the mat, in the manner of a knight throwing down a gauntlet, and said, "Here is my master's signal. There shall be war tonight!" Then he returned to his canoe in haste.

Now there was no time to cook the turtle, for the villagers had more serious tasks to perform in preparing for a battle. Taking their axes, they went off to cut posts to make a fence around the village to protect it from the enemy. All these preparations troubled the child. He was vexed to see the turtle wasted, and he would not listen to his "mother," who tried to explain to him that strange men were coming to fight.

Suddenly, in a loud voice full of authority, the boy said that the turtle *must* be baked. At the same time he gave orders for stems of coconut leaves to be stuck in the ground all around the village for a fence.

"What sort of fence is this?" scoffed many of the people when they saw it. "This will not keep anyone out." But the child took no notice of them, and again in a stern voice he called them to eat the turtle, which was now ready.

"Make haste," he said, "for there is little time before this battle of yours commences."

They had scarcely finished eating before the watchman cried out that fifty canoes were in sight, all full of warriors. So, grasping their clubs and spears, they ran quickly, and they hid until darkness descended.

When the strangers came ashore they were surprised to find no one about, and they laughed heartily at the flimsy fence of coconut leaves. With wild cries they threw their spears—but what a strange thing happened! The spears hit the fence and bounced back! It was as though the fence were bewitched!

Meanwhile, the child made a sleeping potion from strange leaves and had given it to the twin sisters to drink. As soon as they were asleep, he changed himself back to his original size, and once more Wisehead the Giant stood up.

"Ho!" he called out, in a voice that carried across the water to his old home far away. "Tell my grandfather, Longbeard, to send me my war weapons."

Then his grandfather collected clubs and spears, and pulling a hair out of his beard he tossed it into the air. It stretched across the sea, carrying all of the weapons with it.

Wisehead dressed himself hurriedly, adorning his legs and arms with bands of leaves and putting a comb in his hair. Then he took two pieces of kauri gum and stuck them in his armbands and set fire to the gum so that it burned brightly yet without harming him.

He returned for a moment to waken the twins as they slept on their mat, touching them gently with his foot.

"Have no fear," he said, as they started up in a great fright. "I am the small child you found among the banana trees, and now I shall repay you for all your kindness to me. Farewell, for now I go to fight, and then I must return to my own land."

Running toward the fence, he gave a mighty whoop, and when the enemy saw the giant with the flaming torches on his arms, they were terrified and fled back to their canoes. Many fell on the rocks and others plunged into the sea, and when the confusion ended few were left to return to their land and tell the tale of the fierce giant who had defeated them.

THE TWO-HEADED
GIANT OF ROTUMA

Once upon a time there lived in Rotuma a couple with two children, a boy and a girl. Each day the parents went out to work, leaving the children by themselves, telling them to be good and not to open the back door while they were home alone.

One day after the parents had gone, the boy, who was a curious lad, said to his sister, "Let us open the back door and find out what it is that our mother and father wish to hide from us."

So they opened the door, and they found a beautiful garden full of ripe bananas and sugar cane.

"Oh, look at all those good things," said the boy, and he ran and picked a bunch of bananas and cut some sugar cane, and then they both sat down and started to eat.

Meanwhile the mother said to her husband, "Something is happening to the children, for my thumb keeps on itching. I must go and see what it is."

So she returned home and saw at once that the back door had

47

been opened. Picking up her broom, she ran into the garden and found the children eating the fruit. She was very angry, and she started to beat them with the broom. But they ran away.

On and on they ran down a long path, through trees and bushes, till they came to a place where two paths met. They turned along one of them, and presently to their horror they came upon a giant who was sweeping up rubbish, making a clear space in the forest. Quickly they hid behind a tree, but since the giant seemed quite harmless the boy came forward after a time and offered him some of their fruit.

The giant took it and said, "I will give this to my friends. Come along with me."

Now there were ten giants living in that place. When the giants saw the children, nine of them were friendly and would have let them go, but the tenth, who was a two-headed monster, wished to keep them to eat. He took them both to his house and bade them sit down. Then he laid his two heads upon their laps, one head resting on the boy's knees and one head on the girl's, and he told them to comb his hair.

So the children combed the heads gently, and by and by the giant fell asleep. Then, getting up ever so quietly, the children found a rope, bound the giant's arms and legs, and fled down to the shore, where they found a canoe.

"Pick up four large pieces of pumice," the boy said to his sister, while he brought two very heavy stones from the shore and put them in the boat. Then they pushed the canoe into the sea, climbed in, and paddled away with all possible speed.

After a time the little girl grew weary and she looked up at the sky. "I can see a tiny black speck no bigger than a fruit fly up there. Look toward the sun," she said. The boy looked, but neither of them guessed that this speck was the two-headed giant, who had freed himself from the rope that bound him and was flying after them.

It was not long before the giant reached the canoe and stepped into it. The little girl was filled with terror, but the boy said boldly, "Sit down and rest awhile, sir, and watch me."

He then picked up the pieces of pumice and, binding one of the light, spongy pieces to each arm and each leg, he stepped into the sea and began to dance on the surface of the water. This amused the giant so much that he roared with laughter and wished to do likewise.

"Give me your playthings and let me try," he ordered. So the boy got into the canoe and quickly hid the pumice. Then, telling the giant to stretch out his legs, he bound the heavy stones to them. When this was done the boy gave the giant a push. Over he went with a splash into the sea, and the heavy stones made him sink right down to the bottom.

The two children then paddled back to the shore, and they were given the giant's property and his land, where they lived in peace forever after.

MAUI THE FISHERMAN

In the days of long ago the great god Maui became tired of the spirit-land, and so he decided to go on a voyage in search of adventure. The god took with him his two sons, and into his canoe he piled a very long fishing line, to the end of which he attached a magic fishhook. Then they set off to explore the wide Pacific Ocean.

Wherever Maui thought there was land waiting to be brought to the surface he cast his fishhook over the side and let out the line. When he felt the hook strike an object he told his sons to begin to haul, and they strained and pulled with all their might. The first time they were alarmed indeed at the great weight of the fish that they supposed they had caught, and they heaved till the sea bubbled and churned around them. Their canoe rocked so violently that they almost let go of the line, but Maui encouraged them and bade them pull still harder.

Suddenly above the waves there appeared a rocky island and

then another, and, to the surprise of Maui's sons, with every cast of the enchanted hook they brought up either a bare rock or a beautiful coral island.

In this manner Tonga, Samoa, the islands of Hawaii and many others were fished up from the bottom of the ocean floor.

In those far-off days the heavens hung so low that they touched the land, and Maui saw that he must separate one from the other so that there might be light for the world. So he propped up the sky on his shoulders and forced it away from the earth and let in the sunlight upon it.

There was yet another god called Tangaloa. Looking down from the sky, he saw the low-lying islands that Maui had created, and he threw down among them some mountainous ones. Then, seeing so many bare rocks with no sign of life, Tangaloa planted creepers here and there, and soon every island was covered with vegetation. Then he plucked pieces of creeper and left them to dry in the sun, and after a while a worm appeared in the decaying creeper, and that was the first form of animal life.

Then Maui looked down from the sky, where he had returned after his fishing, and, seeing the worm, he changed himself into a bird. Flying down to the earth, he divided the worm into two pieces with his beak, and the old legends say that from these pieces grew the first men.

There came a time when the men grew lonely, and the gods took pity and sent a canoe full of wives for them. The children who were born became the first great chiefs, and they dwelt among the islands and flourished, and their families grew in number.

HOW FIRE CAME
TO TONGA

Now it was long after the peopling of the islands that such a thing as fire was known, and it was brought by the grandson of Maui the Fisherman in this way.

Maui had a son whose name was Maui Atalonga, and every day he left his home in Tonga to visit the spirit-land, and in the evening he returned with cooked food. He did not take with him his young son Maui Kiji-Kiji, nor did he tell him whither he was bound, for the boy was high-spirited and fond of playing tricks. One day Kiji-Kiji determined to find out where his father went, and he followed him to the mouth of a cave hidden by such a dense clump of reeds that he had never noticed the entrance before. He went in cautiously, and finding that the path led to the spirit-land, he followed it, hoping to come upon his father.

At length, when he reached the end of the path, he saw his father digging in a plantation. He crept up behind him, and plucking a fruit from a tree, he bit off a piece and threw it at Maui Atalonga. His father picked it up, was surprised to see the teeth marks, and realized that his son had discovered him.

"Why did you come here?" he said, standing up and leaning on his digging stick. "I forbade you to follow me, for this place is full of dangers. However, now that you are here, you can help me clear this piece of ground. But do not look behind you!"

Kiji-Kiji was delighted. He started to work and pulled up a few weeds, but very soon his curiosity overcame him, and not heeding his father's command, he looked behind. When he did this the weeds grew again, and since he often gave a backward glance, it seemed, by the end of the morning, as if he had scarcely done any work at all, so fast had the weeds grown.

When it was time for Maui Atalonga to cook his afternoon meal he told the lad to go and fetch some fire.

"What is fire, and where shall I go to find it?" said Kiji-Kiji, somewhat mystified.

"Go to your grandfather, and he will give you some" was the reply. So the boy went off and found old Maui lying on a mat by his fire, which consisted of a huge smoldering log from an iron-wood tree.

"What do you want?" said the old man. He was surprised to see a young lad in the spirit-land and did not know that it was his grandson.

"I have come for some fire," Kiji-Kiji replied.

The old man said that he might take some, so Kiji-Kiji gathered up a few of the glowing embers in a coconut shell and took them away. Being a mischievous lad and fond of playing pranks, he blew out the flame on the embers before he had gone many paces, and so he went back and asked for more fire. Old Maui again gave him permission to take some, but again the boy blew out the flame and returned with the same request. By this time the old man was annoyed at having his rest interrupted so often.

"Take the whole of it," he grumbled, and without more ado, his grandson picked up the great ironwood tree trunk and walked away with it.

When old Maui saw this, he realized that he was speaking to no mere human being, and so he challenged the boy to come and wrestle. Then began a wrestling match such as never had been seen before in the spirit world. The old man seized the lad by the cloth that was wound about his waist. He swung him around and around and then flung him to the ground, but Kiji-Kiji was agile as a cat and landed on his feet. Then it was his turn to seize his grandfather. Swinging him around in the same manner, he dashed him to the earth with such force that every bone in the old man's body was broken.

Ever since that fight old Maui has lain feeble and sleepy under the earth, and when the people of Tonga feel an earthquake, they say that he is turning over, and they shout aloud to wake him up lest he should rise too hastily and overturn the world.

Kiji-Kiji returned to his father, who asked him why he had been so long, but the lad refused to say anything. Suspecting that his son had been playing tricks, Maui Atalonga went to see what had happened, and when he found old Maui bruised and hurt he was very angry. He hurried back to punish the boy, but Kiji-Kiji had run away, and he did not come back until evening when it was time to return to earth.

He was then warned by his father that he must not take any fire home with him. But being always full of mischief and unwilling to do as he was told, he tied up some embers in the end of the long piece of cloth that he wore and trailed it after him. They came again to the path leading back to earth, and Maui Atalonga went first. As he neared the end of it he was aware of a smell, and he began to sniff.

"I smell fire," he said.

"I smell none, father," said the deceitful boy, who was following close behind. Just as he reached the end of the path, he untied his cloth quickly and scattered the embers on the ground.

Then a great smoke arose on the land, and soon all the trees were on fire, and it seemed for a while as if the whole earth was in peril. When, after some time, the great fire was quenched, the people managed to keep some glowing embers, so that forever afterward they were able to make a fire and cook their food.

A TRUE LOVE STORY
OF TONGA

Long ago there lived a king of Tonga who was very cruel to his people, and there was much sorrow and unhappiness in the land.

The chief of the island of Vavau wished to free the people of Tonga from the power of this wicked king, but his plan was discovered by a traitor. When the king was informed of the plot against him, he flew into a great rage and ordered that the chief of Vavau be punished.

"I command that he and all his tribe be bound hand and foot and lashed in leaking canoes," he said. He added that these were to be towed out to sea and sunk. The king chuckled at the thought of his revenge.

Now the chief of Vavau had a young daughter named Lifotu. She was a most beautiful maiden, so there was much sadness at the thought of the fate that awaited her and all her family. On a neighboring island lived a young chief, named Toé-umu, who loved Lifotu. He was tall and strong of limb, and upon hearing the king's cruel order he determined to save his beloved.

When night had fallen he went to her house, and calling to her softly so that no one else would hear, he bade her follow him down to the shore where he had left his canoe. The pair sailed away with all speed to an uninhabited island. On that island was a secret cave that Toé-umu had discovered long before, while he had been diving for turtles.

As they neared the shore Toé-umu dived into the sea, bidding Lifotu follow close behind him. They swam under water through a hole in one of the rocks, and rising to the surface they found themselves in a large cave with a dry sandy shore at one end. Toé-umu had often visited this cave secretly, and had hidden mats and food there, thinking that there might come a time when it would be necessary to hide from his enemies.

"Stay here," he said to Lifotu. "This cave must be your home for a while. I will come back soon with more food, but now I must leave you and return to my village before they discover my absence."

Toé-umu paid many visits in secret to his beloved, and though she was sorrowful when she heard the news of the cruel death of all her family, she was content to wait in her cave until she could return with Toé-umu to his people.

After some time had passed, Toé-umu told his friends that he was going to Fiji and would be away a long time. He bade some warriors launch a canoe. When it was ready they came and asked him if he intended to take a wife with him. Laughing, he replied that he would find a wife on the way to Fiji.

When all preparations had been made, Toé-umu and the warriors sailed away toward the little island with the cave. Here Toé-umu, ordering his men to wait for him, dived from the canoe. The minutes passed, and there was no sign of their chief, so the men began to fear that some creature had attacked him. They were about to dive into the sea to search for him when they saw, with surprise and joy, that their chief had come to the surface, bringing with him a beautiful young girl.

"This surely must be a goddess," they said, but as she climbed into the canoe they recognized Lifotu, and they rejoiced to find that she had escaped from the sad fate of her family.

Then Toé-umu and Lifotu sailed onward to Fiji, where the people treated them kindly, and there they remained until the cruel king of Tonga died. Eventually they were able to return to their homeland, where they lived happily ever after.

THE STORY OF
THE SUN-CHILD

Once upon a time there was a great chief in Tonga who had a beautiful young daughter. She was so fair that her father hid her from the eyes of men so that no one could see her, for he had not found a man whom he thought worthy to be her husband.

The chief built a high, thick fence down on the shore. Behind this she was allowed to sit and bathe in the sea every day, until she grew up to be so beautiful that there was no maiden to compare with her.

Now it happened one day that the Sun looked down from his home in the sky and saw her as she rested on the white sand. Immediately he fell in love with her, and after a time a child was born to her, and she called him the Sun-Child.

The child grew and developed into a handsome lad. He was proud and strong, and used to beat the other children as if he were the son of a great chief. One day while all the village lads were playing together on the green he was angered by something, and he picked up a stick and beat them with it until their bodies were sore and his arm ached.

Then they rose up and taunted him, saying, "Who are you, and why should you beat us? We know who are our fathers, but you—you have no father!" At this the Sun-Child was filled with a great rage, and he would have tried to kill them. But he seemed to be rooted to the ground, and his voice became hoarse and his eyes brimmed with tears.

For a moment he stood and glared at them. Then with a loud cry he ran quickly to his own house. His mother was inside, and he seized her by the arm, crying out, "Tell me, mother, who is my father? What do the village boys mean?" And he burst into tears.

"Hush, my son," said his mother, "take no notice of them and do not let them trouble you, for you are the son of a greater chief than their fathers."

"But who is my father?" asked the lad again.

His mother laughed scornfully and said, "Who are those village boys, and why do they despise my son? They are the children of men, but the Sun is your father."

So the Sun-Child wiped away his tears and was happy. "I will not talk to those children of men any longer. I will not even live with them, for I scorn them. I shall go and find my father," he said defiantly.

He called "Farewell" to his mother, and set off without ever a backward glance, and she gazed after him until he was hidden by the bushes and the trees. Through the forest he strode until he came to the beach where his own canoe lay, and at high tide he launched it and sailed away to find his father.

Now it was the early dawn when he hoisted his sail, and he steered toward the east, where the Sun was rising, but as time passed the Sun rose higher and higher, and though the boy shouted loudly his father did not hear him.

Then he tacked and sailed over to the west as the Sun began

to dip toward the horizon, but although he made a fair speed he could not reach his father before he disappeared beneath the waves. The boy was left alone in the wide sea to ponder his next plan.

"My father climbs up out of the water in the east," he said to himself, "so it is there I must go to catch him." He tacked again and sailed eastward all night, and as morning dawned and the Sun rose close to him he shouted aloud, "Look, father, I am here!"

"Who are you?" asked the Sun as it climbed steadily higher.

"Surely you know me! I am your son," cried the lad, "and I have left my mother behind in Tonga. Stay, oh, stay awhile and talk to me."

"I may not stay," said the Sun, "for the people of earth have already seen me. You should have been a little earlier. Now I must go on my way." He bade his son good-bye and rose even higher in the sky.

"Father, stay," cried the lad. "Could you not hide your face behind a cloud and then slip down and talk to me?"

"Truly you are wise, my child," said the Sun, laughing. "For a mere lad you have much wisdom." Then he called for a cloud, and when he had disappeared behind it he slipped down again into the sea. There he met his son and greeted him, and he asked after his mother, and they talked of many things.

"I can stay no longer," he said after a little while, "but listen to me: if you remain here until the darkness comes over the water, you will see my sister the Moon. She is your aunt, so call out to her when she begins to rise from the sea. She has two very precious things; ask her to give you one of them. You must ask for the one called Melaia, and she will give it to you. The other is called Monuia, and you may not have that. Now remember what I have told you and all will be well, but beware of evil if you disobey me."

Then the Sun leaped above the cloud again, and the world

men thought how slowly he was climbing into the sky that day. Meanwhile the Sun-Child furled his sail and lay down on the folds in his canoe and slept until evening. When he awoke he hoisted his sail and waited for the first pale streaks of moonlight. Then he hastened with all speed to his aunt, and he was close upon her before she had risen above the water.

"Luff, luff, child of the earth," she cried out, "or you will pierce my face with the stem of your canoe."

So the Sun-Child altered his steering oar and kept away a point, but he almost touched the moon's face as he passed. Then luffing into the wind suddenly, he shot up alongside her and caught hold of her firmly.

"I am no child of the earth," he said. "I am the Sun's child, and he is your brother, so you are my aunt."

"Oh, are you indeed!" said the Moon. "That is a great surprise, but you are hurting me, nephew, so I beg you to loosen your hold."

"No, no," said the boy, "if I let you go you will leave me, and then you will not give me the present that my father told me to ask for."

"Truly I will not leave you, nephew," replied his aunt. "I am indeed glad to see you, only let me go." So the lad loosened his hold, and then the Moon asked what it was that the Sun had bade him ask for.

Now all this time the Sun-Child, who was a disobedient and high-spirited youth, had made up his mind not to follow his father's instructions. So he said, "My father told me to ask for Monuia."

"For Monuia?" cried his aunt with surprise. "Perhaps, nephew, you have forgotten your father's words? Did he not tell you to ask for Melaia?"

"No, he did not," the lad replied indignantly. "He said I might have Monuia, and that you were to keep Melaia."

This is strange indeed, thought the Moon. Surely my brother cannot hate the boy and wish to harm him, and yet I must obey his commands. Then aloud she said to her nephew, "Very well, you shall have Monuia. It is only a little thing and wrapped in a piece of cloth. See, I will put it inside yet another wrapping and I will bind it around and around many times to make it firm so that it cannot come open by itself. Take it now, and I implore you to remember my words. Do not undo the wrapping and take out the present while you are still at sea. Now away with you, and set your sail for Tonga, and I warn you once more not to look at Monuia until you have landed or a terrible evil will befall you."

She bade him good-bye and climbed upward in the sky, giving her pale light to many. The mariners at sea welcomed her, and the children in the villages came out of their houses and started to dance on the grass.

Then the Sun-Child steered for Tonga and sailed for two nights and a day, until on the morning of the second day he saw land. Then he could wait no longer, for he was an impatient lad and self-willed. So he took up the parcel that his aunt, the Moon, had given to him and untied the string. He unrolled each fold of cloth until at last he held Monuia in his hand.

It was a most beautiful pearl shell of an unusual red color. Such a one had never been seen before, and it shone in his hand as he gazed at it. He thought how fine it would look as an ornament hanging around his neck, and how all the boys would envy him.

At that moment he heard a mighty noise like a rushing and a splashing over the water. He looked up and saw from every side a great throng of fishes swimming toward him. There were fish of every kind, and great whales and sharks, porpoises and dolphins and turtles, and they leaped upon him in their eagerness to reach the shell. So great was their weight that his little canoe sank beneath the waves, and the Sun-Child was seen no more.

RATA'S CANOE

There was once a chief named Rata who lived long ago in the spirit-land of Kupolu. He longed to explore distant lands, and so he decided to build a great double canoe. Shouldering his ax, he set off to a valley where the tallest trees grew. On his way he passed a stream. Here, by a pandanus tree, he came upon a fight between a beautiful white heron and a spotted sea snake, and he paused to watch the deadly combat.

The heron had been fishing by the sea and, growing weary, had perched on a rock to rest. This annoyed the sea snake, who lived in a hole under the rock, and he resolved to catch the heron. He put his head out of the water to see in which direction it flew, and then he pursued it with all haste. Swimming to the mouth of the stream, he followed its course until he came to the pandanus tree where the heron was asleep. Since the tree had many roots growing from the base of the trunk and stretching down into the water, the snake was able to climb up. Holding on by twining

66

his tail around a root, he attacked the bird and began to bite it. It was at this moment that Rata passed by, and the heron called out to him for help.

"O Rata, put an end to this fight," the bird cried.

But the deceitful snake said, "Nay, Rata, leave use alone. It is but a trial of strength. Leave us to fight it out."

Since Rata was in a hurry to fell timber for his canoe, he went on, but as he turned away he heard the heron say reproachfully, "Your canoe will not be finished without my aid." And again it asked for help.

But Rata walked on until he found the timber he sought. After cutting down enough for his boat, he returned home at sunset. Early the next morning he set off, intending to hollow out the trees he had cut. But, strange to say, he could not find his logs. Not a lopped branch, or chips, or fallen leaves, could be seen. Neither could he see any stumps, for the trees had been mysteriously restored to their upright position. Nothing daunted, he felled them a second time and then went home.

On the third morning as he went to the forest, he passed the heron and the snake, who were still fighting. For two days and nights they had not ceased their battle. When Rata reached his trees he found that again they were standing boldly in their original positions. Now he remembered the words spoken sorrowfully by the heron: "Your canoe will not be finished without my aid."

He ran back quickly to the scene of the fight, and he found that the beautiful bird was almost exhausted and that the sea snake was about to deliver the final blow.

Rata gripped his ax, and swinging it with all his might, he chopped the cruel snake into many pieces, setting the heron free. Then he went off to cut down his trees for the third time.

When the heron revived, it came and perched on the branch of a tree and watched Rata's labors. At sunset, as Rata returned home, the grateful bird flew off to collect all the other birds of Kupolu, and throughout the night they worked hard, pecking away at the logs to hollow them. Then the sea birds who had the longest bills bored the holes, and the land birds secured the bindings with their strong claws. It was almost dawn before they completed their task. Finally the heron called them all to lift the canoe and carry it to the beach by Rata's dwelling. Then every bird, large and small, settled on one side of the canoe or the other, each putting one wing underneath to raise the craft, while using the other wing for flying.

As the birds flew to the beach they sang this song:

> Make way for the canoe,
> Clear a path for the boat,
> Take it through trees,
> Bear it through flowers.
> The birds of Kupolu
> Honor Rata our chief.

Awakened by the unusual singing of so many birds, Rata collected his tools and was about to return to his trees when he caught sight of the canoe lying outside his house. He was amazed by the beauty of the work and guessed that it had been done by the birds, although not one could he see, for they had disappeared into the forest.

He then made a mast and a sail, and he named his canoe "Taraipo," which means "built in a night." Then he collected food and water, and he called his friends to accompany him.

When all was ready, a crafty magician appeared and asked if he might sail with them, but Rata refused to let him come on board. Then secretly the magician seized a large coconut, and knocking a hole in it, he squeezed himself inside and floated off in the sea, following the canoe. By and by Rata's men saw the nut bobbing before them, and one man stooped down and picked it up out of the water. He found it very heavy, and peering into the hole, he was astonished to discover a small man inside it.

"Take me with you, O Rata," said the magician, still inside the coconut.

"Whither away?" inquired Rata.

"To the land of Moonlight, to seek my parents."

"Well, what will you do for me in return?" asked the chief.

"I will look after your mat-sail."

"I have enough men to attend to the sail," said Rata. "I do not want your help."

After a while, still crouched inside the coconut, the magician again asked to be allowed to remain on board in order to sail to the land of Moonlight.

"What else can you do for me if I take you with us?" Rata inquired.

"I can bail out the water from the bottom of your canoe," he replied.

Again Rata said, "I do not want your help. I have plenty of men to bail out water."

Yet a third time the magician pleaded, offering to paddle the canoe whenever the wind dropped, but Rata still refused to take him.

At last the tiny man said that he would destroy all the monsters of the ocean that might trouble them.

Rata now became interested, for he had forgotten to provide against any such emergency, and wisely he permitted the magician to remain on board. Growing suddenly to his normal size, the man took his place at the forepart of the canoe, and he kept a sharp lookout for monsters.

At first they sailed swiftly over the water, with a fair wind filling the sail, seeking new lands. Then one day the magician called out, "O Rata, beware, here is a fearful enemy."

It was a giant clam. So great was the size of the shell that as it opened one half of it lay ahead of the canoe and the other half lay astern, threatening the vessel with the danger of being crushed when it closed. But the magician seized his long spear and drove it deep into the clam's flesh, so that, instead of crushing them all in its shell, the creature sank slowly to the bottom of the sea.

Continuing their journey, the men soon let down their guard, but the sharp eyes of the magician spied another foe.

"O Rata," he shouted, "yonder comes a terrible octopus."

The monster had already encircled the canoe with its huge arms and threatened to pull it under the water, but again the magic spear was thrust forward and it pierced the evil-looking head. At once the arms relaxed their grip and the octopus drifted away, mortally wounded.

One more peril lay in wait for the voyagers. This time a great whale came toward them with its jaws wide open, and the men thought their last moments had come.

The resourceful magician now broke his long spear in half, and just as the whale was about to swallow them, he thrust the two stakes upright inside its mouth, so that it was impossible for the jaws to close. Then he jumped down into the great mouth and looked right into the whale's stomach. There he saw his long-lost father and mother, who had been swallowed alive when out fishing one day.

His parents, who were busily plaiting a rope, were overjoyed at seeing their son, and he promised to rescue them immediately. Jumping into the whale's open mouth, he quickly removed one of the stakes propping it open and broke the stake in two. Then, by rubbing the pieces together briskly, he made a spark that set fire to the blubber in the whale. Writhing in agony, the monster swam swiftly toward the nearest land, and when it reached a sandy beach, the three passengers walked out of its open mouth and escaped.

All this time Rata and his men had followed them, and they landed on the same beach. They all lived peacefully on that pleasant land for a year. At length they decided to return home, and after repairing the canoe and collecting food and water, they set off once more.

This time the voyage was completed without any perils or terrors, and sailing toward the setting sun they reached their homeland in safety.

THE COCONUT TREE

Long ago, in a faraway coral island set in the warm blue Pacific Ocean, there lived a beautiful maiden called Ina. She had raven-black hair and brown skin, and she lived with her parents in a house made of reeds with a thatched roof. Near her home there was a fresh-water stream in which there were always plenty of fish and large eels. It flowed swiftly over boulders and pebbles, and formed deep pools, and finally disappeared beneath the rocks.

Each day at dawn and sunset, Ina left her house and went to bathe in one of the pools near a clump of trees. One day a huge eel, larger than any she had ever seen, swam upstream from its hiding place beneath the rocks and startled her when she felt it touch her foot. But the eel did her no harm, and it returned so often that Ina became accustomed to seeing it and was no longer afraid of the creature.

One day as she watched it, to her great surprise the eel changed into a handsome young man.

"Do not be afraid of me," he said. "My name is Tuna, and I am the god and protector of all fresh-water eels. I have loved you for a long time, and I have now left the dark rocks where I live to try and win your love."

From that day he became her suitor. He changed into a young man whenever she came to visit him but turned into his old form of an eel when he returned to the stream.

There came a day when Tuna declared, "I must leave you now." But before he said good-bye to the maiden he told her that he would leave a wonderful gift so that she would always remember him.

"Tomorrow there will be a storm, and the rain will cause the stream to overflow and it will flood the valley. Do not be afraid, for I will swim up to your house on the hill, and when you see me in the form of an eel I will lay my head on your wooden doorstep. Cut off my head at once and bury it. Then go every day to look at the place, and wait and see what will happen."

Ina was very sad to think that she would see him no more, and she went slowly home. That night it rained and rained, and the noise on the roof was like thunder. She remembered what Tuna had said, and at dawn she looked outside and saw that the floods had indeed covered the valley and all its plantations and gardens, and that the water was just lapping the edge of her house. At that moment a large eel appeared. It swam right up to the entrance and laid its head on the doorstep. Ina ran and fetched her chopper made from a sharpened shell, and sadly she chopped off the eel's head. Then she buried it quickly on the hillside near her house.

After a while the rain ceased, and the waters drained away to a mere stream once more. Every day Ina visited the place where she had buried the head, but there was nothing to be seen. Then one day she found a tall green shoot growing, and each day it grew and grew and sent out long leaves.

By and by when it had become a tall tree, it flowered and bore fruit in the form of large clusters of nuts. When they were husked Ina found that on each one were marks like Tuna's two eyes and mouth. He had kept his promise and left a gift in memory of his love for her. Her people also found that it was indeed a wonderful gift, for the tree had so many uses. The nuts gave them food and drink, and the leaves could be plaited by the villagers to make mats and fans and also sails for their canoes. With the leaves they thatched their houses, and as time went on they found many more uses for the trees that grew from those first nuts.

As time passed, it became the custom that whenever anyone went sailing from one island to another he would throw a nut into the sea. "Perhaps some starving shipwrecked man will need this nut," the traveler thought, "or perhaps it may grow upon some other island." And to this day the people of the Pacific still throw a coconut overboard whenever they travel by sea.

HOW INA
TATTOOED THE FISH

Long ago there lived a fair maiden called Ina. Her parents were wealthy, for they possessed many beautiful shells which they wore as jewelry and a fine headdress made from scarlet and black feathers. These ornaments were put out to air in the sunshine regularly, and they were guarded with care.

One day the parents left their home, bidding Ina mind the treasures. But an evil spirit named Ngana, who was lurking behind the bushes, overheard their conversation. Waiting until the father and mother were out of sight, he came to Ina and begged to see the ornaments, and then he asked to try them on. With soft words and crafty ways he adorned himself in all the finery, last of all adding the feathered headdress. Then he began to dance all around the house, for Ina had taken him indoors to prevent him from escaping. However, he spied a hole in the roof, and flying up through it he disappeared forever.

Not long afterward the parents returned, and when they discovered the loss of their treasures they were very angry with Ina. They beat her with sticks and branches of trees until the weeping girl ran down to the beach to escape from their rage. Her two brothers followed her, but she bade them farewell and declared that she would try to find Tinirau, the lord of all the fishes.

Now Tinirau lived on the Sacred Isle, which lay toward the setting sun. Ina gazed wistfully over the ocean, wondering how she could reach his island. Looking about, she noticed a small fish, the Avini, swimming by her feet.

"Ah, little Avini," she cried to him, "are you an ocean-loving fish? Bear me on your back to Tinirau, and he shall be my royal husband."

The little fish consented to take her, and Ina sat herself on its narrow back. But it had not gone far before it found her too heavy, so it turned over and tipped Ina into shallow water. Angry at this wetting, she struck the Avini again and again, and the stripes on the side of the little fish are still there to this day.

Returning to the shore, she looked about for a larger fish, and very soon a Paoro came near her, and he said he would be pleased to take her on this romantic voyage. Again Ina proved too heavy. The Paoro dropped her off his back and swam away, but not before Ina had struck him angrily and left blue marks upon him. He and his descendants still keep the marks, and like the Avini's stripes, they have been called "Ina's tattooing."

Then a white fish appeared, but even this one was unable to carry Ina, and she turned him completely black to mark her disgust at the third failure.

She now tried another fish, a sole, and together they reached the edge of the breakers before she was tipped off the fish's back. This time, in her rage, Ina stamped on the head of the unfortunate sole with such energy that the eye on the underside came through to the upper side. Ever since that day the sole has had to swim flatwise, because one side of its face has no eye!

Then, far out in the deep water, a shark came in sight, and Ina called to it and begged it to take her to the Sacred Isle. When the great fish swam close to her, she mounted its broad back, taking with her two coconuts to eat on the journey.

When they were halfway across the sea she felt thirsty, so the shark raised up its dorsal fin, and on this Ina pierced the eye of one of her nuts and drank the milk. After a while she again felt thirsty and asked the shark for help. This time the shark lifted its head, and Ina cracked the hard shell on its forehead. Smarting from the blow, the shark dived into the depths of the ocean and left her floating in the sea, and ever since then he has carried a bump on his forehead.

The king of all sharks then came to rescue Ina, and after many more adventures she reached the Sacred Isle and went ashore. Here she was surprised to find salt-water ponds full of every sort of fish, and slowly she made her way to Tinirau's dwelling. Finding no one in the house, she beat gently on a drum that stood nearby. The noise of its booming reached Tinirau, who was over on another island, and he returned with haste to his home.

Ina saw him nearing, but suddenly being overcome with shyness, she hid behind a curtain. Tinirau could find no one, and was about to set off once more when Ina beat again on the drum. This time Tinirau found the maiden. Enchanted by her beauty, and hearing of her courageous voyage to find him, he fell in love with Ina and made her his wife.

Ina then lived happily on the Sacred Isle with her husband, the lord of all the fishes; and in the course of time she bore him two children, a boy and a girl.

LASA AND THE
THREE FRIENDLY SPIRITS

There was once a man named Lasa who dwelt on Vavau island in Tonga. One day he went out into the bush to cut down a tree to make a canoe. After a whole day of toil a tree was felled and Lasa went home to sleep. During the night the god Haelefeke, who was half octopus, came to the felled tree and said to it, "Lasa's tree, stand upright," and all the chips of wood flew together and the tree stood up again in its place. In the morning Lasa came and spent another whole day in felling the tree. That night, while he slept at home, the Octopus came again and restored the tree to its place. This happened three times. After hewing down the tree for the fourth time, instead of returning home Lasa hid himself and lay in wait. This time when the Octopus came Lasa sprang out and seized him and held him until he had promised to help build the canoe. So they built the canoe together, and when Lasa was preparing to sail away in it, the Octopus said, "If you should see anyone beckoning to you, do not refuse to take him with you."

Lasa set sail, but after he had gone a little way he saw some-one beckoning to him from the shore. So he stopped and took this man on board, and it happened to be the Hungry Spirit. A little farther on he saw someone else beckoning, and went to him, and took on board the Thieving Spirit; and still farther on he found the Octopus himself and took him on board as well.

Then they sailed away to Fiji and landed on an island where a demon lived. They smoothed out their footprints in the sand, hid the canoe, and went to the demon's house. Lasa climbed up to the ridgepole of the house, while the three spirits each stood close to a post. The demon was not home, but he presently returned, bring-ing weeping people whom he had stolen. At once he began to sniff suspiciously, saying, "I smell the smell of humankind," and catch-ing sight of Lasa, he hauled him down from his perch. Then he saw the three spirits and tried to pull them out into the open, but the Octopus clung so tightly to his post that the demon could not pull him away; indeed, his hauling seemed likely to pull the house down. So the demon asked the Octopus to let go his hold on the post and promised that he would not harm him.

The demon brought in food, saying, "If you do not eat up every bit of this, you shall surely die." The Octopus and the Thieving Spirit both ate as much as they could, but still the food was not nearly finished. "Hungry Spirit, you must save us," said Lasa. So the Hungry Spirit saved them by devouring the huge meal and, finally, the leaves and the bowls that the food was brought in.

The demon then told them that he was going to shake his vi tree, and that they would die if any of the fruit fell to the ground. Lasa looked up and saw that the tree was so laden with fruit that not a single leaf could be seen. "Now surely we shall die," he mur-mured sadly, but the Octopus saved them by spreading himself out under the tree and catching all the fruit with his tentacles, so that not one escaped him.

After this the demon thought of yet another way to outwit the strangers. He called one of his Fijians and told him to go with the Thieving Spirit to gather land crabs, and that they were to have a race. "This time nothing shall save your lives," he shouted, "unless you can beat my man." So the two went off, and as the Fijian knew the place well he had his basket filled before the man from Tonga had caught even a single crab. As they were about to return, the Thieving Spirit asked the Fijian to climb a coconut tree to get nuts for them to drink. When the Fijian was up in the tree, the Thieving Spirit began to sing, "Tongan wakeful eye, Fijian sleepy eye; Tongan wakeful eye, Fijian sleepy eye." And he kept on singing until the Fijian fell asleep in the tree. Then the Thieving Spirit quickly filled his own empty basket with coconut husks and exchanged it for the Fijian's basket of crabs. Having done this, he woke the Fijian, who came down from the tree and seized the basket of husks, not knowing that it had been exchanged. When the trick was discovered the demon flew into a great rage, and he told Lasa and his three friends to leave quickly and return to their own land. They obeyed immediately, and Lasa journeyed home without any further dangers.

THE RAT AND
THE SQUID

There was once a man called Manu-Manu who built himself a fine big canoe. When it was finished he thought he would like to go on a journey, and he looked around for a few creatures to accompany him.

First he asked the frigate bird to come. It replied that it would, and asked if it might bring along its friends.

"What will you do if my canoe sinks?" asked Manu-Manu.

"We will fly," said all the birds in chorus.

Then he went to the land creatures, and he spoke to the crab, asking him to come on the journey. The crab said he would come and would bring his relatives with him.

"What will you do if my canoe sinks?" asked Manu-Manu again.

"We will crawl along the bottom of the ocean," said the crab and all his relatives.

Now the rat crept up, and he begged to be taken on the voyage with them. "I will swim if your canoe sinks," he said. So Manu-Manu agreed to take him, and they all embarked in the canoe and set sail.

All went well at first, but after a time the canoe sank in a rough sea. The birds of the air flew homeward, and the land creatures crawled along the bottom of the ocean. But the rat swam. He swam until he was so tired that he could scarcely swim any more. Then a squid came by and peered at him with an inquisitive glance. The rat jumped quickly onto its head and begged the frightened squid to carry him to land, where the rat's grandparents and family lived.

By this time he was very hungry, so he nibbled the hair off the squid's head.

"What are you doing, rat?" said the squid.

"Oh, nothing," said the rat. "Go on swimming a little farther, since I can see the shore and we are almost there."

So the squid swam on until they were close to the land and the rat was able to jump ashore.

"Good-bye, squid," called the rat as he watched his benefactor making for the ocean once more. And then he shouted, "Oh, squid! Feel your head; it's bald!"

The squid felt his head and found that it was quite bald; and being very angry at the rat's trick, he turned and swam back to punish him. The rat, however, had run away inland. So the squid went back to the sea, and he waited and watched each day for the rat to return.

By and by the rat came down to the shore again, and looking about for food he went into a crab hole. The squid thrust one of his tentacles into the hole to catch him, but the rat, too quick for him, turned and bit off the end. Then the squid put out another tentacle; and this time it went right into the rat's ear and killed him.

From then on, because of the trick that the rat had played on the squid, the squid taught his children and his grandchildren to chase all rats. That is why, to this day, the people on many islands use bait that is shaped like a rat when they want to catch squids. It is made from the backs of two brown cowrie shells, bored and tied together with thongs, and it even has a small shell for the head and a wooden tail.

HOW THE YAM CAME TO
THE NEW HEBRIDES

Once there was a young man named Kaloris who lived on Vila island. One evening he went out with his bow and arrows to shoot a flying fox, which is really a kind of bat and good to eat. He was proud of his bow, for it was the finest in the village, and none of the men could shoot an arrow so far or so straight as he. With the fox bat he had shot, he returned to his village at midnight. Strolling along the beach in the moonlight, he wondered suddenly what the land on the moon might be like. An idea came to him: it would be an adventure to go and see the moon for himself!

He stopped in his tracks as he thought of a plan. Then, laying his bundle of arrows on the sand, he took one up and fitted it to his bow. Pointing it at the moon, he took careful aim, drew the string right back to his shoulder, and let it go. The arrow sped as swift as the wind, up and up, until it reached the moon and stuck there firmly.

Kaloris took a second arrow, and again he fitted it to his bow and took aim very carefully. This time the arrow pierced the shaft of the first, just as he had planned, and he was proud of his marksmanship. He shot a third and then another and another, until he had a long line of arrows, each one sticking into the one before it. They stretched from the moon right to the beach where he stood.

Then he put down his bow, and seizing the lowest arrow he climbed upward until at last he reached the moon itself. There was a large trap door on the underside of the moon, so he knocked on it.

"Come in," said a voice. So he pushed open the door and went inside.

There he saw the Man of the Moon, eating his food.

"Good health to you," said Kaloris.

"Good health," said the Man of the Moon. "Where have you come from?"

"I have come from Vila, and I have climbed up here by a ladder of arrows," said Kaloris, and he explained how he had shot them into each other.

"Come and share my food—you must be hungry," said the Man of the Moon.

Kaloris thanked him, and he sat down and joined the Man of the Moon at the meal. He enjoyed what he was eating, for it was new to him.

"What is this that we are eating, sir?" he asked.

"That is a yam," said the Man of the Moon. "Surely you have some on your island?"

Kaloris said that he had never heard of a yam. So the Man of the Moon pointed to a big pile of them lying in a corner and told him to take as many as he wanted.

Then, opening the trap door, they pushed out the yams one by one, and they fell down to earth and landed on the beach where Kaloris had stood with his bow and arrows.

When he had thanked the Man of the Moon he bade him farewell and climbed down his ladder of arrows and returned home. His friends, curious about the strange food, crowded around him, and taking the yams home they planted them in their gardens. Soon they had a fine harvest, and all of the people said it was the best food they had tasted; and that is how yams came to the New Hebrides.

HOW THE MASI DIVED
FOR A SUNBEAM

Long ago there was said to be a tribe of people called the Masi who lived in the Solomon Islands. They were noted for their foolishness and ignorance.

One day six of the Masi fishermen found some bait that could be used for catching porpoises, so they decided to launch a small canoe and go fishing. Paddling the boat swiftly, they kept a lookout for a porpoise, singing as they went along.

After a little while one of the men looked down into the water beneath him, and there he saw a sunbeam.

"Friends," he said, "there is a beautiful shining pearly ornament down there. Let us try to get it. Now then, back water with your paddles and do not make too many ripples on the surface."

They followed his bidding and then sat very still. Gazing into the depths, they saw the sunbeam, and each one thought it was a mother-of-pearl shell.

"I will dive down and get it," said the leader. So the rest kept their paddles stiff to steady the canoe, and he jumped into the water, but, alas, he could not reach the bottom. Then each one tried in turn, but not one of them was able to reach the sunbeam, for the water was too deep. Back they paddled to the shore, and there they searched for large stones with holes in them, and for long pieces of tough creeper, and these were put into the canoe. Then they paddled back once more to the place where they had seen the sunbeam.

"There it is, comrades! Steady the canoe, and I will go down," cried the leader. He tied a large stone to his foot and told the men to wait a long time for him to come up, for it might be difficult to gather up the ornament in his arms. They lowered him over the side, and down he went, deeper and deeper—but he never came up again. They waited about, watching the bubbles float up to the surface, and told each other that he was certain to get it. He was gone such a long time that the second man said, "I will dive down also and give him a hand." So he too tied a stone to his foot and dived into the water, while the rest waited for the two to return. When neither of them came up with the prize, the others went down one after the other.

Not one of the foolish Masi came to the surface again, and none of them lived to tell their friends of the beautiful sunbeam at the bottom of the sea.

Tales from the South Pacific Islands

Designed by Barbara Holdridge

Composed by the Service Composition Company, Baltimore, Maryland
in Bookman with Reef display

Printed by the John D. Lucas Printing Company, Baltimore, Maryland
on 70 lb. Howard Textbook Opaque White

Bound by the Complete Books Company, Philadelphia, Pennsylvania
in Kivar 5 Limeade, Linenweave